THE STORY OF PASSOVER

The first Passover happened long ago in the far-away country of Egypt. A mean and powerful king, called Pharaoh, ruled Egypt. Worried that the Jewish people would one day fight against him, Pharaoh decided that these people must become his slaves. As slaves, the Jewish people worked very hard. Every day, from morning until night, they hammered, dug, and carried heavy bricks. They built palaces and cities and worked without rest. The Jewish people hated being slaves. They cried and asked God for help. God chose a man named Moses to lead the Jewish people. Moses went to Pharaoh and said, "God is not happy with the way you treat the Jewish people. He wants you to let the Jewish people leave Egypt and go into the desert, where they will be free." But Pharaoh stamped his foot and shouted, "No, I will never let the Jewish people go!" Moses warned, "If you do not listen to God, many terrible things, called plagues, will come to your land." But Pharaoh would not listen, and so the plagues arrived. First, the water turned to blood. Next, frogs and, later, wild animals ran in and out of homes. Balls of hail fell from the sky and bugs, called locusts, ate all of the Egyptians' food.

Each time a new plague began, Pharaoh would cry, "Moses, I'll let the Jewish people go. Just stop this horrible plague!" Yet no sooner would God take away the plague than Pharaoh would shout: "No, I've changed my mind. The Jews must stay!" So God sent more plagues. Finally, as the tenth plague arrived, Pharaoh ordered the Jews to leave Egypt.

Fearful that Pharaoh might again change his mind, the Jewish people packed quickly. They had no time to prepare food and no time to allow their dough to rise into puffy bread. They had only enough time to make a flat, cracker-like bread called matzah. They hastily tied the matzah to their backs and ran from their homes.

The people had not travelled far before Pharaoh commanded his army to chase after them and bring them back to Egypt. The Jews dashed forward, but stopped when they reached a large sea. The sea was too big to swim across. Frightened that Pharaoh's men would soon reach them, the people prayed to God, and a miracle occurred. The sea opened up. Two walls of water stood in front of them and a dry, sandy path stretched between the walls. The Jews ran across. Just as they reached the other side, the walls of water fell and the path disappeared. The sea now separated the Jews from the land of Egypt. They were free!

Each year at Passover, we eat special foods, sing songs, tell stories, and participate in a seder— a special meal designed to help us remember this miraculous journey from slavery to freedom.

This
PJ BOOK
belongs to

_____

_____

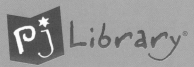

PIPPA'S PASSOVER PLATE

by Vivian Kirkfield
illustrated by Jill Weber

Holiday House · New York

Hurry, scurry,

Pippa Mouse,

washing,

scrubbing,

cleaning house.

Passover starts at six tonight,
Seder meal by candlelight.

Hustle, bustle, lots to do.

Pippa stirs a chicken stew.

Sets the table—all looks great.

Where's the special Seder plate?

HAGGADAH
HAGGADAH

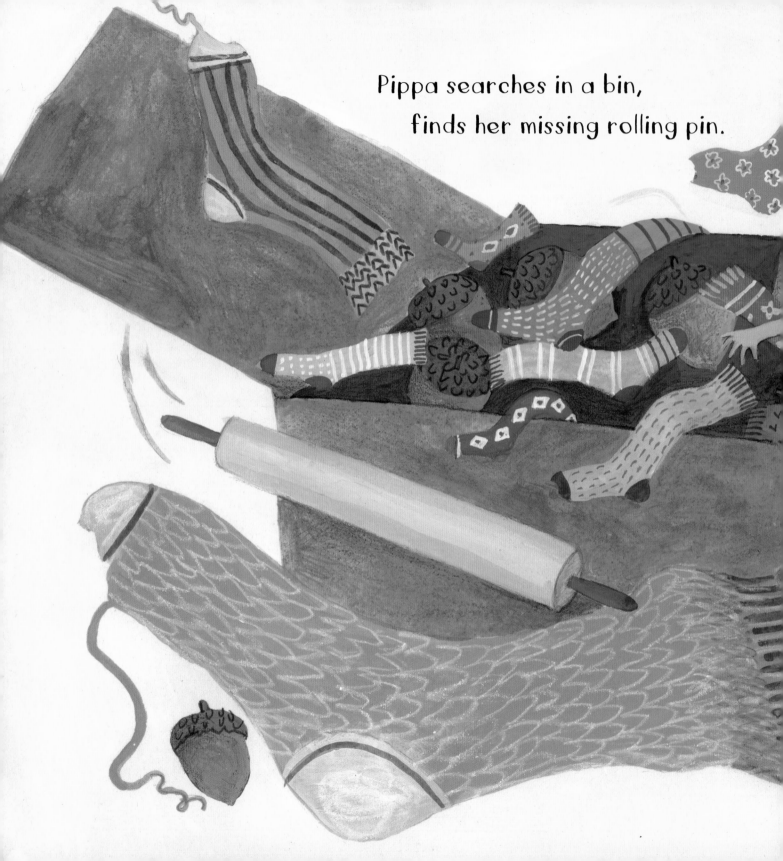

Pippa searches in a bin,
 finds her missing rolling pin.

Pippa opens up a box,
filled with eighteen holey socks.

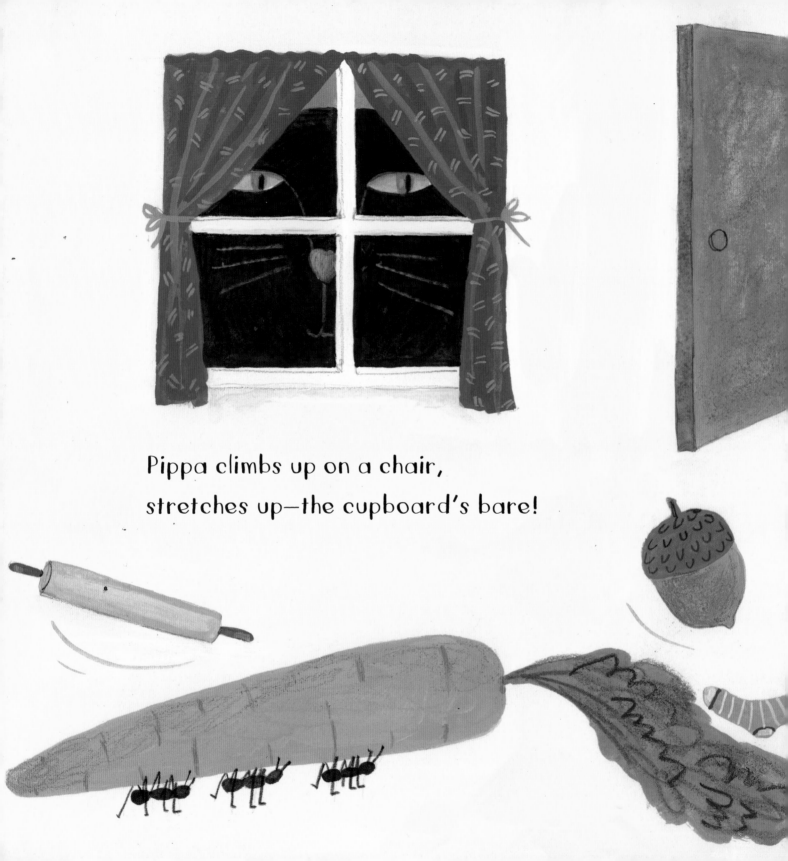

Pippa climbs up on a chair,
stretches up—the cupboard's bare!

Teeter-totter—hold on tight!
Weeble-wobble—what a fright!

Pippa runs out to the yard.
Sphinx, the cat, is standing guard.

QUIVER! QUAVER!
SHIVER! SHAKE!

Cats make Pippa cringe and quake.

Pippa, though afraid to stir,
gently strokes the velvet fur.
"Have you seen my Seder plate?
Sun sets soon—it's getting late."

"No," purrs Cat.
"Go ask the snake,
    slither-sliding
        near the lake."

QUIVER! QUAVER!
SHIVER! SHAKE!

Snakes make Pippa cringe and quake.

Pippa scrambles down the lane.
Offers Snake a daisy chain.
"Have you seen my Seder plate?
Sun sets soon—it's getting late."

"No, I haven't," Snake replies.
"Go ask Owl, she's old and wise."

QUIVER!   QUAVER!
SHIVER!   SHAKE!

Owls make Pippa cringe and quake.

Stumble, tumble down the trail.
Pippa prays she will not fail.

In a quiet woodland glade,
Owl sits in leafy shade.

"Have you seen my Seder plate?
Sun sets soon—it's getting late."
"No, I haven't seen the dish.
Why not question Golda Fish?"

Golda loves to primp and preen.
She was once a beauty queen.
Seder plate is made of brass,
shining like a looking glass.

At the water, near the edge,
Pippa climbs up on a hedge.
Thinks she spies a golden fin...
Splash! Poor mouse has fallen in!

At the bottom—
something round.

Can you guess what Pippa found?

Ball and coin and old tin can,
bottle cap and rusty pan,
globe to circumnavigate.
Best of all—the Seder plate!

Fish swims up with mouse in tow.
To the Seder all will go.

Pippa and the others cheer.
Life is good when friends are near.

BEITZAH
a hard-boiled egg

ZEROAH
a roasted bone

KARPAS
sprigs of
parsley or
onion or
boiled potato

MAROR
horseradish
root

CHAZERET
Romaine lettuce

CHAROSET
a mixture of chopped
apple, walnut, and red
wine

SEDER *PLATE*

To my village of critique partners,
you know who you are, and especially Jill,
who fell in love with Pippa and
brought her to life
V. K.

For Rainer, Sterling, Jack
& Charlotte
J. W.

HOLIDAY HOUSE is registered in the U.S. Patent and Trademark Office.
Printed and bound in October 2018 at Toppan Leefung, DongGuan City, China.
The artwork for this book was created with acrylic gouache and Neocolor crayons with a bit of collage.
www.holidayhouse.com
First Edition
3 5 7 9 10 8 6 4 2
ISBN: 978-0-8234-4453-3 (PJ Library edition)

Library of Congress Cataloging-in-Publication Data
is available on the Library of Congress website.
031927.5K1 / B1351 / A3